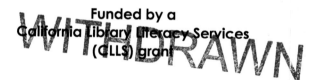

Bed and Breakfast

Quick Reads

**Funded by a
California Library Literacy Services
(CLLS) grant**

RIVERSIDE
PUBLIC LIBRARY

GAIL ANDERSON-DARGATZ

Bed and Breakfast

Grass Roots Press

First published in 2013 by Grass Roots Press

Grass Roots Press gratefully acknowledges the financial support for its publishing programs provided by the following agencies: the Government of Canada through the Canada Book Fund and the Government of Alberta through the Alberta Foundation for the Arts.

Grass Roots Press would also like to thank ABC Life Literacy Canada for their support. Good Reads® is used under licence from ABC Life Literacy Canada.

Library and Archives Canada Cataloguing in Publication

Anderson-Dargatz, Gail, 1963–, author
    Bed and breakfast / Gail Anderson-Dargatz.

(Good reads)
ISBN 978–1–77153–000–2 (pbk.)

    1. Readers for new literates. I. Title. II. Series: Good reads series (Edmonton, Alta.)

PS8551.N3574B43 2013   428.6'2   C2013–902651–7

Printed and bound in Canada.

For Vincent, my own handyman

Chapter One

I waved goodbye to my first guests of the summer. My busiest season had just started. I run a bed and breakfast in my big old house. Travellers rent my bedrooms, and I serve breakfast in the morning. I love welcoming visitors, but I don't do it for fun. Without my paying guests, I would have to sell my home.

The couple I was waving to was about my age, in their mid-forties. The man put a hand on his wife's back as he opened the car door for her. Joe, my husband, used to do that for me, before he died.

After the couple drove away, I stood on my porch, thinking of my husband. Joe was a handsome man who took pride in his appearance. Every Saturday night, we went out to dinner together. We often walked along the lakeshore later in the evening. We always stopped and kissed under the stars.

But Joe was killed in a car accident five years ago. I had been alone ever since. Now I wanted to share dinner with someone. I longed for a man to talk to during the long nights of winter. I wished now for the kind of romance I had shared with Joe.

I was lonely, but I wasn't alone. I had friends. In this small town, everyone looked out for everyone else. Steve was my closest friend. Before Joe passed away, Steve was his best friend. Now that Joe was gone, Steve watched over me.

In any case, this morning I didn't have time to feel sorry for myself. I had dishes to wash and beds to make. I knew at least one new guest would arrive that day. A man named Brent Henderson would stay overnight at my bed and breakfast.

I turned to get ready for my guest and walked right into Steve. "Steve!" I said, "You surprised me." As always, he had come in through the kitchen door at the back without knocking. I hadn't heard him walk through the house to the front porch.

Steve was dressed in his grubby work jeans and T-shirt. His brown hair was a mess. There was stubble on his chin. He usually came to my place to repair something. Today, he looked the same as he always did, ready to get to work.

Steve grinned and held out a handful of lilacs. "Here you go, Annie," he said.

I took the flowers. "For me?" I asked him.

Steve brought me something from his garden nearly every day. I knew his gifts were an excuse for a visit. He also pretended to forget his tools at my place a lot. That way he could come back, pick up his tools, and have another chat over coffee.

But this was the first time he offered me flowers, so I was a little worried. Steve and I were old friends. I didn't want him to think we were anything more than that.

He must have seen the concern on my face. "I thought you might like flowers for the guest rooms," he explained.

I blushed. I felt silly for worrying that the lilacs were just for me. "They're lovely," I said. "Thanks."

Steve and I went inside the house. I ran some water into a vase for the lilacs. Then I poured cups of coffee for Steve and me. We sat at the kitchen table to drink them and talk.

"So I'm fixing the leak under the sink today?" he asked me.

I nodded. Steve was the best handyman in town. He could fix anything that was broken. My house was a hundred years old. Guests said it had "character." In other words, it needed a lot of work. Steve had to repair something almost every week.

"I sure appreciate everything you do for me," I said.

"You pay me well enough," he said. "Besides, what are friends for?"

Steve and I were friends, good friends. We were best friends. That is, until Brent Henderson arrived.

Chapter Two

After I did my chores, I helped Steve with the plumbing under the sink. We had almost finished taking the old pipes apart before putting in new ones. I was on my hands and knees beside Steve when I heard an unfamiliar voice, a man's voice.

"Hello?" he said through the screen door of the kitchen.

I jumped, bumping my head under the sink. "Oh!" I said, holding the back of my head.

A *very* handsome man stood at the screen door. He was so good-looking that he could have been a movie star. His hair was blond and his eyes sparkled blue. Something about him made me feel both thrilled and nervous.

"I knocked at the front door, but you didn't hear me," he said. He opened the screen door and came into the kitchen. "I phoned yesterday. I booked the night here." He carried an overnight bag.

Now I knew who he must be. "Mr. Henderson," I said. I got up off the floor and offered him my hand. We shook hands before I realized that slimy stuff from the old kitchen pipes covered my fingers.

"Call me Brent," he said. He looked down at his hand. It, too, was now dirty with slime.

"Oh, god, I'm so sorry," I said. Already I had embarrassed myself in front of my attractive guest.

Brent looked disgusted. I gave him a towel, and he wiped the slime off his hand. He wore an expensive suit and a colourful shirt and tie. No one dressed like that in our town.

I felt very poorly dressed next to him. I wore jeans and a T-shirt with a silly happy face printed on it. What would such a stylish man think of me?

"I didn't catch your name," Brent said as he handed back the towel.

"I'm Annie. Annie Clark."

I couldn't take my eyes off Brent. He was tall, with broad shoulders, and he carried himself with confidence. He was clean-shaven and smelled good. Expensive aftershave, I thought.

Steve was on his knees at my feet. He smelled like the slime in my old kitchen pipes. He looked like a plumber. When he saw me staring at Brent, he cleared his throat so I would notice him.

"Oh, and this is Steve," I said.

"Steve Armstrong," Steve introduced himself. Without standing up, he held out his hand to Brent. Slime from the pipes also dirtied Steve's fingers. He knew it, too.

Brent paused a moment before shaking Steve's hand. He didn't want to get his hands dirty again. But he shook Steve's hand anyway.

I handed Brent the towel again and apologized for Steve. Brent wiped his hands once more. "The drive up here from the city went faster than I expected," he said. "There wasn't much traffic. This town is pretty quiet, too, isn't it?"

I nodded. "For now," I said. "The tourist season is about to start."

For most of the year, our town is so quiet that deer, rabbits, and foxes live here with us. They walk up the roads and come right into our yards. Then, in June, the tourists arrive. People travel here for the sandy beach and the sun. They come for the peace they don't find in the city. Then they drive their motorcycles back and forth along our quiet country roads.

"This is a great place to relax," I told Brent. Then I couldn't think of anything more to say. I just stood there, gazing at Brent like a love-struck teenager. Brent's eyes were such a pure, clear blue that I wondered if he was wearing coloured contact lenses.

Brent looked from me to Steve and back again. He smiled as if he thought we were very strange. I imagine we did look odd to him. We were two country bumpkins, staring at this handsome stranger from the city.

"May I see my room?" Brent finally asked me.

Steve elbowed me in the leg to get me to respond. "Yes, yes, of course," I said. "This way."

Chapter Three

Brent picked up his overnight bag and followed me down the hall. I put him in the largest guest room. The room had a queen-sized bed, a dresser, and a desk. My guests shared the main-floor bathroom. If they wanted to watch TV, they joined me in the living room.

"I hope this is all right," I said.

"It's perfect," he said. "It's exactly what I pictured." He put his bag on the bed. Then he looked around at the flowered wallpaper. "I feel like a kid on vacation at Granny's house."

I was sure Brent didn't mean to insult me. I didn't take his comment that way, anyway. The house was old, so I had decorated it with antiques, flowered wallpaper, and matching bedspreads. The house was charming, but it did look like a granny's house.

"Your towels are here," I said. I pulled out the top drawer of the dresser. "If you forgot to pack anything, let me know. You'll find toothpaste and shampoo in the guest bathroom just down the hall."

"That's wonderful," he said. "Thank you."

He was politely sending me away. I knew I should have left the room at that moment. A good bed and breakfast host gives her guests privacy. But I felt drawn to the man. I struggled to think of something to say so I could stay with him a little longer.

"Perhaps you'd like an extra pillow," I said. Then I felt silly. There were already four pillows on the bed. "No, these are fine," Brent said.

"Well, let me know if you need anything," I said.

"Thank you, I will."

As he turned to look out the window at the lake, I glanced at myself in the dresser mirror. I had a huge black streak of slime from the sink pipes on my cheek. I quickly tried to rub it off. That only made it worse. I now looked like I had a black eye.

Brent smiled when he turned from the window to find I was still there. I saw him notice the black under my eye, but he didn't say anything about it. I knew Steve would have pointed it out. Brent, on the other hand, had manners.

"I take it Steve is your husband?" Brent asked.

I laughed. "No, no," I said. "Steve is just here to fix the sink."

"My mistake," Brent said. "You seem very comfortable together."

"We've known each other a long time," I said. "Steve was my husband's best friend."

"Your husband passed away?"

I nodded. "He was killed in a car accident. A driver fell asleep at the wheel and ran into him."

"I'm so sorry."

Brent looked so sad for me that I felt myself start to cry. But I brought my emotions under control. "The accident was a long time ago," I said.

"I just lost my wife this winter," Brent said. "She died of breast cancer."

"Oh, no," I said. I felt the tears return. I knew what losing a spouse was like. But I also thought, So, he's single.

"That's why I'm here," Brent said. "I just had to get away from our house in Toronto. Too many things there remind me of my wife."

I nodded. I understood. There were reminders of my husband all over my old house, even in that very guest room. There was the trim Joe had nailed around the doorway. There was the light fixture he had hung up. Joe and I had papered the walls together.

"I know exactly how you feel," I said. "I sometimes feel like Joe is still here with me."

"You never remarried?" Brent asked.

"No." Brent's eyes were *so* beautiful. When he gave me his full attention, as he did now, I felt warmed inside, but also shy. "I don't get many chances to meet new people here," I said.

"Except during tourist season," Brent said. He winked at me. His smile made my heart beat faster. Was he saying what I hoped he was saying? Could he possibly be interested in me? I said a hasty goodbye and left the room before he could see me blush.

Chapter Four

I went back to the kitchen and wiped my face clean with a paper towel. I checked in the mirror over the sink to make sure I had removed all the black stuff. My face was still dirty. No, I thought. A man like Brent Henderson could not possibly be interested in me.

"Well, I just made a complete fool of myself," I told Steve. I meant talking to my guest with slime on my face. But that wasn't what Steve heard.

"Couldn't keep your eyes off him, eh?" Steve asked.

I looked down at Steve. He was still kneeling, working under the sink. "I was that obvious?" I asked. If Steve had noticed my interest, Brent must have noticed it, too. Heat rose up my neck and over my face. I was blushing.

Steve sat back to look up at me. "I suspect he's used to women staring at him," he told me. "He's the kind of man who wants that sort of attention. Look at him. All dressed up like that."

"Shush," I said. "He might hear you." I glanced back down the hall to Brent's room. "Anyway, I like how he dresses. I appreciate a man who keeps himself clean-shaven and tidy."

"Like Joe did," Steve said. I paused, thinking of my husband. "Yes, like Joe." My husband shaved every morning. He ironed his own shirts. He worked at a bank, so he wore a suit to work every day. But he was gone now.

Steve ran a hand over the stubble on his chin. He seemed to think about what I had said for a minute. Then he stuck his head back under the sink. "Brent isn't a plumber, that's for sure," he said. "What does he do for a living?"

"I don't know. He didn't say where he worked."

"He probably sits at a desk all day. I couldn't live like that. Imagine being shut up in some office building in the city. I would feel trapped."

Normally, I would have agreed. I didn't want to live in the city. But I wasn't really listening to what Steve was saying. I looked back in the mirror.

"Look at me," I said, mostly to myself. I rubbed more dirt off my face. "I didn't even put on makeup today." How could a man like Brent possibly find me attractive? I felt dowdy in that moment, middle-aged, with no sense of style.

But then Steve said, "A woman as beautiful as you doesn't need makeup."

I was stunned. Steve had never said anything like that to me before. "You think I'm beautiful?" I asked him.

He bonked his head on the underside of the sink as he turned to look at me. His face was red. He was embarrassed, too.

"Of course you're beautiful," he said. "Didn't you know that?"

No, I thought, I didn't.

I looked back at myself in the mirror. My hair was messy from working under the sink. I still had a little black slime on my face. But I did have lovely green eyes. My reddish brown hair framed my pretty, heart-shaped face.

Even though I had already turned forty-five, I looked as if I was still in my thirties. I didn't have any grey hairs. My figure was still trim because I walked or biked nearly everywhere I went. Steve was right. I guess I was pretty good-looking for my age.

"You're not just beautiful," Steve said. "You're smart and funny." Steve hid back under the sink. "Brent would be lucky to have you," he muttered.

I saw myself differently then. I was beautiful, and I was smart, too, about some things at least. When my husband died, I had turned our home into a bed and breakfast to support myself. I used my computer to promote my business on the internet. People from all over the world saw my ads on websites and came to stay here. Some of my guests came back every year.

Steve was right. Brent *would* be lucky to have me, I thought. I would just have to help Brent figure that out for himself.

Chapter Five

Brent wandered back into the kitchen as I wiped the last of the slime off my face. When I saw him smile at me in the mirror, I quickly stepped away from it. I was embarrassed that he caught me looking at myself again. I tried my best not to look at Brent, either. When I snuck a glance at him, he smiled at me, clearly amused by my behaviour.

He clapped his hands. "So, what do people do for fun around here?" he asked.

"Fun?" said Steve. He looked up at Brent from under the sink. "We haven't had any fun around here since 1985."

"He's joking, of course," I said. Then I played host and told Brent what I usually told my guests. "You could drive over to Bridal Falls," I said. "The waterfall is lovely. Or you could head into town to shop."

"Or you could just take a hike," Steve said. I gave him a warning look. He seemed to be telling Brent to get lost. I should have known then that something was up. Steve wasn't behaving like himself; he was rarely this impolite.

I tried to smooth over Steve's rudeness. "Yes, there are many places to hike," I told Brent. "Or you could take a quiet walk on the beach. The water is just a few steps down that way." I pointed towards the front door and the road that led down to the lake.

"I think I'll do that," Brent said. "Thanks." He glanced at me, smiling. "Too bad I don't have someone to keep me company," he said. Was he really asking me to join him?

I watched as Brent strolled through the front door. He turned and smiled at me again. He gave a little nod towards the beach before he finally left. He was clearly asking me to follow him there.

I couldn't believe my good luck! Nothing could inspire romance like a walk on the beach. This was my chance to show Brent just how beautiful and smart I really was.

I ran to the bathroom and quickly dabbed on eye shadow and mascara. I didn't need blush because I was blushing enough already. Once I put on a little lipstick, I was done.

When I rushed back into the kitchen, Steve glanced up at me and away, then immediately looked at me again. He whistled. "You're all dolled up."

"What are you talking about?" I said. "I haven't even changed my clothes."

I was embarrassed that Steve noticed I had put on makeup. Brent would, too, then. Would Brent think I was trying too hard to impress him?

I took a last look at myself in the mirror. "Think you can finish putting the sink together by yourself?" I asked Steve as I patted my hair into place.

"Oh, I think I can handle it," he said. Then I realized that he had already finished the job and was cleaning the cupboard under the sink. That was my job. I knew then that Steve was taking his time, waiting to have coffee with me. We often drank another cup after he finished fixing something.

"I can't stay and chat right now," I told him. "Catch you later?"

"Yeah, sure," he said. He sounded disappointed and a little hurt.

I hesitated as I watched him put the cleaning rags back in the pail and get up off the floor. I didn't want to let Steve down, especially knowing everything he did for me. But I couldn't pass up this chance at romance with Brent. I headed towards the front door.

"Where are you going in such a hurry?" Steve called after me. I didn't answer him. His voice told me that he already knew.

Chapter Six

I walked to the water and turned down the beach. I hoped to catch up with Brent, but he was already a long way ahead of me. I couldn't get closer without running after him. If I did that, I would look too eager to spend time with him. So I took my time strolling along the sandy beach. We would run into each other when he turned to come back, I thought.

The water was shallow in the bay. Sunlight reflected off the sandy bottom and made the water appear green in places. Even though our town was in Northern Ontario, the shore looked like a tropical beach. The water was cold, though. I wouldn't try to swim in it until well into July.

I reached Brent at the end of the beach. Instead of turning around, he had sat on the boulder that I often sat on. Dressed in his fine suit, he looked out of place. He must have guessed what I was thinking because he looked down at himself. "I should have changed first," he said.

"No, you look charming," I said. Like a fashion model posing for a photographer, I thought. "Am I intruding?"

"No, not at all. I'm glad you came." He moved over on the boulder to give me room to sit. "I told you I wanted company." He grinned, and I felt a thrill run through me. I sat next to him.

"The beach is lovely," he said. He waved a hand at the lake in front of us. "I understand why you choose to live here."

"My late husband brought me here," I said. "He got a job at the local bank, so we bought that house."

"Your bed and breakfast," Brent said.

"Yes, though we never thought of turning it into a B&B at the time. We didn't think we would stay more than five years. I thought we were too cut off from everything out here. But then I got used to the quiet. When my husband died, I didn't want to leave."

"You mean you didn't want to leave the life you built with your husband," Brent said.

I looked at him, surprised. "Yes," I said. He understood my feelings perfectly.

Brent didn't say anything more. He seemed lost in thought, and I was lost for words. Brent made me feel clumsy, unsure of myself. We sat in silence for a long time.

"Well, I should let you have your peace and quiet," I said finally. I was disappointed at how my brief visit with Brent had gone. I stood to leave.

"No, don't go," he said. "Please stay."

He looked so sad as he begged me to stay. I hesitated a moment, not sure how to react.

"I thought I wanted to get away from the noise of the city," he said, to explain himself. "But now that I'm here, I'm stuck with my own thoughts."

"Your memories of your wife," I said.

"Yes."

I sat back down on the rock beside him. We watched the waves lap the shore at our feet.

"Winter is the hardest time for me," I said. "I'm okay in the summer. My house is full of guests. I'm busy making beds, cooking breakfast, cleaning house."

"But when the house is quiet ..."

"Then I think about Joe, my husband," I said. "I get so lonely."

"I sometimes turn to tell my wife something, but she isn't there," Brent said.

"I used to do that all the time," I told him.

He took my hand and squeezed it. "It's good to talk to someone who understands."

I looked down at his hand holding mine. Brent Henderson was holding my hand! I wanted to hold his hand forever. I wanted to start a new life. With him. I looked up at his face, wondering if that was a possibility. But he was gazing at the lake as if he was looking into the past.

Chapter Seven

When Brent and I arrived back at my bed and breakfast, Steve was gone. The old sink pipes were in the garbage can, and the floor around the sink was washed. Steve hadn't left even one of his tools behind. That meant he wouldn't come for a visit that evening, as he often did on Saturday nights. I felt disappointed.

Then I cheered myself with the thought that Brent was there. He would stay the night in my home. I planned to ask him to sit with me in the living room later on, as guests sometimes did. I felt that if we spent more time together, his obvious feelings for me would grow. However, I never expected what happened next.

"Is there a place to eat dinner in this town?" Brent asked me.

I thought briefly of suggesting the fish and chip shop where Steve and I sometimes had supper. But Brent was dressed in a suit. I suspected he had a different sort of restaurant in mind. A fine-dining restaurant was in order.

"The Old Church Restaurant is just up the road," I said. "The food there is excellent."

"Would you care to join me?" he asked. My heart skipped a beat. Brent must have seen the shock on my face. "I hate eating alone," he explained. "Honestly, I haven't enjoyed a meal since my wife passed away."

I knew what he meant. Meals were the loneliest times, even meals eaten at home. I hated eating by myself in a restaurant.

"Of course, I understand if you don't feel it's appropriate," he said. "Or if you feel having dinner with me would upset Steve."

I laughed a little. "Steve?" I asked. "Why would he care?"

Brent shrugged. "I thought you and he might be dating. The way he looks at you…" He didn't finish his sentence.

How had Steve looked at me? Sometimes I caught Steve watching me, but he quickly looked away.

"Steve and I aren't dating," I told Brent. "As I said, he's just a friend."

"Well, then, how about dinner?"

I tried to sound relaxed, even though I was so excited I wanted to jump up and down. "I'd like that," I said. "Just let me get changed." But what was I going to wear?

I ran upstairs and searched my closet for something dressy to put on. I found jeans and pants. I pushed back the messy line of blouses, blazers, summer dresses and coats hanging in the closet. There had to be a nice dress in there somewhere.

Then I found it. Forgotten and hanging in the back was a little black dress. The dress was sleeveless; only thin straps held it up. If the dress still fit, it would show too much skin and too much cleavage. That was exactly what I was looking for.

But would the dress fit?

I took off my jeans and T-shirt and slid the dress on over my head. I struggled to get into it. The dress was just a bit tight. I had put on a few pounds in the past five years. But I managed to get it on.

I kicked my sandals and runners out of the way and hunted for my shiny black high-heeled shoes. I slipped them on. Then I rummaged through my jewelry box until I found my fake-diamond earrings.

When I was fully dressed, I stepped in front of the mirror. "Wow!" I said to myself. The little black dress hugged my womanly curves. I hardly recognized myself.

Brent just happened to walk out of the bathroom as I was coming downstairs. He stopped and stared up at me. "You look absolutely wonderful," he said.

That was my Cinderella moment. I felt like the cleaning girl transformed into a princess by her fairy godmother.

But then my heel caught on the bottom step and I fell down. I landed on all fours right at Brent Henderson's feet.

Chapter Eight

"Shit," I muttered as I got up off the floor. So much for my Cinderella moment.

Brent helped me up. "Are you all right?" he asked me.

"I'm fine." I laughed to cover my embarrassment as I brushed off my little black dress. "I haven't worn high heels in a long time," I said. "They take a little getting used to."

"Well, then," Brent said, offering me his arm. "Let me help you keep your balance."

I put my arm through his, feeling both foolish and excited. Here I was, walking arm-in-arm with such a gorgeous man! He led me to the front porch. I kept my mind on getting down the steps without falling again.

The evening was pleasant. The sun shone, though I could see a few storm clouds building. We never know what kind of weather we might get here. The sky can be clear one hour and dark with rain the next.

"You say the restaurant is within walking distance?" Brent asked as we reached his car.

"Yes, just up the road."

"Shall we walk, then?" He grinned at me. "Or are you up to it?"

"I think I can manage," I said. But as soon as I said that, I slipped on the gravel under my high heels. I smiled at him, hoping he wouldn't notice my embarrassment.

"Are you *sure* you can manage?" Brent asked. He actually looked concerned.

I nodded, blushing. "I'll be fine," I said. Those damn shoes weren't going to stop me from having a romantic arm-in-arm stroll with Brent.

Once we were on the pavement, I found walking easier. But I knew I would have blisters on my heels when I got home.

Our town is very small. Everyone knows everyone. On that sunny June evening, almost all my neighbours were outside enjoying the weather. Many were making supper on their barbeques.

They watched Brent and me as we walked up the road arm-in-arm, all dressed up. They stared at us, in fact.

Brent smiled and nodded at them. For the most part, they seemed too stunned to say anything, even hello.

"Friendly town," Brent said, glancing at me. His face told me that he meant my neighbours were anything but friendly.

"They don't mean to be rude," I told him. "They don't often see a man as handsome as you." I lowered my voice as I added, "*I* find it hard not to stare."

"Well, thank you," Brent said. "But they're not looking at me."

I glanced back at my neighbours. Brent was right. My neighbours weren't staring at Brent. They were staring at me.

I looked down at myself, to make sure my dress still covered what it should. It showed a little too much cleavage, all right, but that was on purpose. "I guess they're surprised to see me in this dress," I said. "I rarely have a reason to dress up."

Brent shook his head. "No," he said. "That's not it. I think they are staring because they don't often see a woman as beautiful as you."

Okay, *that* was my Cinderella moment. I felt like a princess. I had to look away from Brent because I couldn't stop grinning.

As we passed Steve's house, Steve left his barbeque to watch us pass by. He still had his flipper in his hand. He had been using the flipper to turn hamburgers on his grill when he saw us.

I waved at Steve and Brent nodded at him. "Hello, Steve," Brent said. "Fine evening."

Like my other neighbours, Steve said nothing, at first. He just watched us walk by with a look of shock on his face. Once we passed by his place, I heard him call my name. "Annie," he said.

I turned back to look at him.

"I told you," Steve said. "You *are* beautiful. And he *is* lucky to have you." He waved his flipper at Brent and spoke directly to him. "I just hope he knows it."

Chapter Nine

As we walked to the restaurant, I glanced at Brent to see how he reacted to what Steve said. I was afraid Steve had scared him off. But Brent didn't say anything about it, not right then.

When we arrived at the restaurant, he opened the door for me. We went inside. The restaurant building was an old church. Stained glass windows dimmed the light in the room. Each table held a lit candle. Everything about the place was perfect for creating a little romance. I hoped that was still possible.

The hostess led us to our seats. She took our drink orders and left us menus. I couldn't stand it anymore. I had to say something to Brent about what had just happened. "About what Steve said—," I started.

"That I'm lucky to have you?" Brent asked. He smiled at me, and I suddenly felt foolish for saying anything at all.

"Yes, that's it," I said. I paused. I wasn't sure what else to say. I didn't want Brent to think I was expecting too much of him.

"It's okay," said Brent. "Don't think anything of it. It's clear Steve has feelings for you."

"It is?"

"Of course." He looked at me, puzzled. "You don't see it?"

In that moment I saw Steve's actions in a whole new light. I knew he was leaving his tools behind so he had an excuse to visit. But now I realized why. To him, we were much more than friends. The lilacs Steve brought me that morning *were* for me, and not for my guests.

But his romantic intentions weren't welcome. I really liked Steve, just not in that way. I couldn't see him, grubby in his work clothes, taking me out to dinner as Brent did now.

"He wants you, Annie," said Brent. "He sees me as a threat. It's okay, I understand. Don't let it ruin our evening together."

"No, of course not."

"The chicken looks good," he said, looking at his menu.

"Yes, it does. I think I'll have that."

The waitress came to take our dinner orders. "Shall I order for you?" Brent asked me. "Please." I was delighted. My husband had ordered for me when he took me out to fine restaurants. I couldn't see Steve doing that. When Steve and I ate lunch at the fish and chip shop, he and I paid for our own meals.

"You live in the city, in Toronto?" I asked Brent, after the waitress left.

"Yes," he said.

"Steve was wondering what you do for a living."

"Steve wondered, did he?" Brent smiled. He was amused. He knew I was the one who really wanted to know.

"He guessed you weren't a plumber," I said.

"No." Brent smiled. "You can tell Steve I own a gallery."

"A gallery?"

"I sell works by Toronto artists: painters, photographers, sculptors, potters."

"Expensive stuff, I imagine," I said.

"We deal only in the very best."

"We?" I asked. Did I have competition? A woman he worked with, perhaps?

"I run the gallery with my brother," he said.

"Ah," I said, relieved.

"My wife was a painter," he said. "That's how we met. I sold her work."

My heart sank. There was no way I could compete with the ghost of his wife. She was an artist, a city woman who knew all about culture. All I did was run a bed and breakfast in a sleepy little town.

"I suppose I seem simple by comparison," I said. As soon as I spoke, I wished I could take the words back. Brent now knew I was comparing myself to his dead wife. Worse, he knew I was hoping for more than just a dinner with him. I was asking for too much, too soon.

"Not at all," Brent said. "You're refreshing. I feel very at ease with you."

But something shifted between us. Brent was charming all through supper, yet he also kept his distance. He smiled more at the pretty waitress than he did at me.

I knew my chance at romance with Brent was over. At least, I thought it was. Then the rain began, and everything changed.

Chapter Ten

The rain poured down in sheets. Water quickly gathered into pools on the pavement. Streams of water ran down the road.

"What the hell?" Brent said as we left the restaurant. "The sun was shining before we ate."

"Just a regular day around here," I said, holding my purse over my head. "We better make a run for it."

I slipped my high heels off and ran down the street in my bare feet. When Brent didn't follow right away, I took him by the hand and urged him on. We ran down the street hand-in-hand, laughing.

Steve had been watching the downpour from his doorway with a beer in his hand. Then he saw Brent and me running through the rain together. He stepped inside and closed the door behind him.

Brent and I were soaking wet when we reached my bed and breakfast. "I haven't had that much fun in a long time," Brent told me. "You make me feel like a kid again." He kissed me on the cheek.

Then he headed down the hall to his room. "I've got to get out of these wet clothes," he said.

I was thrilled. Brent had kissed me! He did have feelings for me after all.

I went upstairs and changed, too, into pants and a T-shirt. Then I started a fire in the downstairs fireplace, thinking it would entice Brent into the living room. The room soon warmed up from its glow.

I sat in my favourite red chair in front of the fire and put my feet up. I sipped a glass of wine and attempted to look both at ease and stylish. When Brent came in, I wanted him to think I looked like a city woman.

But he didn't come back to the living room right away. As I waited, I shifted my position in my chair, trying to look sexy.

"Brent," I called finally. "Care to join me in the living room for a nightcap?" I figured the offer of a glass of wine would encourage him to join me.

When he didn't answer, I walked down the hall to his room to ask him again. I was about to knock on his door when I heard Brent turn on the shower in the bathroom down the hall.

I turned away, disappointed. I imagined he was having a shower before bed, and that was the end of our date.

But then I heard Brent yelp. "Shit!" he cried, as if he was in pain. I heard the shampoo bottle fall into the bathtub. The shower curtain rattled open as he jumped out of the shower.

"Brent," I called through the bathroom door. "Are you all right?"

Brent turned off the shower taps and opened the door. Dressed in his white bathrobe, he could have been a model in a shampoo commercial on TV. That is, he would have looked like a model if he wasn't both shocked and angry.

"There was no hot water!" he said. "My shower was freezing!"

"Oh, I'm so sorry," I said. "I'm not sure what could have happened. Did you turn on the hot water tap?"

"Well, of course I turned on the hot water tap." He waved at the shower angrily, inviting me to check things out for myself.

I turned on the tap and felt the stream of water, which was icy cold. "You're right," I said. "There is no hot water."

"Believe me, I know," said Brent. The skin on his face and hands was pink from the cold shower.

I turned on the sink tap. No hot water there. Brent followed me into the kitchen. No hot water there, either.

"I imagine there is something wrong with the hot water tank," I told him. "I wonder if I can simply turn up the heat."

"I have no idea," Brent said. "If I have any kind of problem at my place, I phone my building superintendent."

"Your superintendent?"

"He takes care of the apartment building where I live," Brent said. "He's kind of like your Steve," he added. "If something breaks, I phone him."

Steve, I thought. Of course! Steve would know what to do. I ran to the phone.

Chapter Eleven

Steve knocked on the front door. Usually he just walked right in. He nodded hello when I opened the door, but he didn't smile. He went straight to the kitchen and I followed. Once there, he turned on the hot water tap and felt the stream of water, just as I had.

"See?" I said. "Nothing but cold comes out."

Steve opened the electrical box on the kitchen wall and checked the breakers. They all looked fine. "The hot water tank is still getting power," he said. "So something has gone wrong with the tank. I'll go down into the basement and take a look at it."

I went back into the living room to wait for him. Brent sat in my favourite red chair, warming himself by the fire. He still wore his bathrobe.

"I don't think you're going to get your hot shower tonight," I told him. I held up the bottle of wine. "Can I make up for it by offering you a glass of wine?"

"Of course," he said. "And all is forgiven."

I handed him a glass and refilled my own.

Brent and I were sitting together sipping our wine when Steve came into the living room. He had cobwebs in his hair from the basement. He glanced at Brent, and at Brent's bathrobe, but didn't say hello. Then he turned to me.

"Your hot water tank is nearly as old as I am," Steve told me. "That thing should have been replaced decades ago. Not worth fixing."

I sighed. "I suppose now I've got to buy a new hot water tank?"

He nodded. "I'll pick one up from the hardware store tomorrow."

"Thanks, Steve."

Steve took one more look at Brent in his bathrobe. "I'll let you two get back to whatever you were doing," he said. He looked angry. I could see that he thought Brent and I were sharing a lot more than just a bottle of wine.

"I'll see you out," I said.

"No need," Steve said. "I know my way."

I walked with him to the front door anyway. When we got there, I lowered my voice so Brent wouldn't hear. "There was nothing going on between Brent and me," I told Steve. "He was having a shower when he discovered we had no hot water."

"What you do in your own home is none of my business," Steve said.

"Then why do you look so angry?" When Steve didn't answer right away, I said, "Brent thought you and I were married. Then he thought you and I were dating." I paused. "Can you imagine?"

I admit I was testing Steve, to see what he thought of that idea. But right away I regretted what I said. I knew by the look on Steve's face that I had hurt his feelings.

"Obviously *you* can't imagine us dating," he said. He turned to go.

"Steve," I said. "Wait." But he stormed off and disappeared into the night.

Brent was right. Steve wanted me, and he did see Brent as a threat. I wondered if I had just lost my best friend.

I went back inside the house. Brent was still in the living room, drinking his wine. "Everything all right?" he said.

"Yes, yes," I said. "Everything is fine."

"Steve was angry, wasn't he?"

"He had no reason to be angry."

"He wasn't too pleased to see me in my bathrobe."

"Think nothing of it," I said. I tried to sound casual. "I want my guests to feel at home here."

Brent leaned forward and took my hand. "But I'm more than just a guest, aren't I?"

I felt weak in the knees from his touch. Yet for the first time that day, I wasn't sure I wanted Brent's attention. Not if that meant I would lose Steve's friendship.

"I feel that we are kindred spirits," Brent told me.

"Kindred spirits?"

"We've been through similar things," he said. "I lost my wife, you lost your husband. We understand each other in a way others don't."

Steve understands me, I thought. Better than anyone.

Brent leaned back and crossed his ankles again. "Steve sees that connection between you and me. He's jealous of it."

Yes, I thought, I know. But how could I fix things between Steve and me?

Chapter Twelve

Steve knocked on the front door again in the morning. I knew then that he was still mad at me. But I was determined to mend our relationship. I wanted our friendship to be as strong as it was before Brent arrived.

When I opened the door, I said, "You know you don't have to knock."

"This isn't my house," he said. "Walking right in would be rude."

"That never stopped you before," I said. I smiled, hoping to lighten his mood. He ignored my remark and went straight to the basement door. He would have to haul the old hot water tank up the stairs before putting the new one in.

"Wait," I called, before he went downstairs. "Don't you want a cup of coffee first?" We always had a coffee and a chat before he started a job around the house.

"I've got other things to do today," he said. "I expect you do as well. I assume you're spending the day with your Mr. Henderson?"

"We have no plans. He's hardly *my* Mr. Henderson."

"Where is he, anyway?" asked Steve. "He hasn't already left, has he?"

"He went for a walk on the beach," I said.

"Without you?"

"He asked me to join him," I said. "I told him I was waiting for you to arrive."

"To put in the new hot water tank."

"Well, yes."

Steve grunted as if I had said the wrong thing. "I was looking forward to seeing you, too," I added. But Steve still looked upset.

Steve was cleanly shaven for the first time I could remember. His chin was smooth and free of beard stubble. He smelled good, of Old Spice aftershave. He had never used aftershave before.

"You look nice today," I said. "You smell nice."

"I see you're all dressed up today, too. For that Mr. Henderson, no doubt."

I glanced down at myself. I had on what I thought was a casual outfit, pants and a blouse. But the outfit was dressy compared to what I usually wore around Steve.

"Did you do something with your hair?" he asked me.

"I blow-dried and styled it this morning," I said. "Do you like it?"

"I liked you better before," Steve said. "You were all natural."

"Thanks a lot."

"I didn't mean to insult you," he said.

"You could use a haircut," I told him. "You would be a good-looking man if you took care of yourself."

"So you're saying I'm not much to look at now."

"I didn't mean it that way," I said.

"Is that how you see me, as just some slob? Is that all I am to you, the grubby local handyman?"

"No," I said. "You're my friend."

"Your *friend*?"

"Yes. You're my good friend, my best friend. I don't want to do anything to risk that." I poured him a cup of coffee and handed it to him. "I can see you're angry with me," I said. "I'm just not sure why."

The look Steve gave me suggested that he didn't believe me. "Think about it," he said.

I shook my head. Of course, I did know why he was angry with me. I just didn't know what to say.

"Why do I bring rhubarb or salad greens over every day?" he asked me. "Why do I forget my tools here? Why do I find excuses to visit you?"

I held my hands out. "We're friends."

He put his coffee cup down on the kitchen table without taking a drink. "We *were* friends," he said, before turning back to the basement. "We're not anymore."

Chapter Thirteen

Brent arrived back at the bed and breakfast just as Steve was leaving. The two men danced from side to side at the front door, trying not to run into each other. Finally, Steve grunted in disgust and pushed past Brent. He stomped off up the road to his house.

"He's in a terrible mood this morning," Brent said as he came in.

"We had an argument," I explained.

Brent followed me to the kitchen. I banged dishes around in the sink as Brent leaned against the kitchen counter. "I think I can guess what your argument with Steve was about," he said. "I imagine I'm the problem?"

"None of this is your fault," I said. "I handled things badly. I hurt Steve without meaning to. I simply didn't realize he felt that way about me."

"Well, it's time for me to head home, anyway. I'm sure Steve will be in a better mood once I've left."

I looked into Brent's perfect face. "Do you have to go?" I asked him. "Couldn't you spend another couple of days here? We've only just started to get to know each other."

"I have to open the gallery in the morning," Brent said. "My brother is away. He can't fill in for me tomorrow."

"When will I see you again?" I asked.

"I'm sure our paths will cross down the road." He said the words so casually, as casually as he would say them to any stranger. I knew then that I would never see him again.

I turned away. I felt rejected, hurt. "But I thought . . . I thought there was something between us."

Brent put a hand on my arm, so I would look at him. "Annie, you're so beautiful, and the time I spent with you yesterday means everything to me."

"But . . .," I added, when he paused.

"But I've just lost my wife. I'm not ready to get involved with anyone. I thought you understood that. I thought you felt the same way."

I did understand. When I first lost Joe, the last thing I wanted was to find someone new. That was a long time ago, though. I was ready for a relationship now.

"I feel so foolish," I said.

Brent pulled me to him and hugged me. "Please don't feel that way," he said. "This is my fault. I'm aware of the effect I have ..." He paused again.

"On women." I finished the sentence for him.

"Yes. I should have been more careful with your feelings," he said. "I just found you so comfortable to be around."

Comfortable, I thought. I didn't want Brent to find me comfortable. I wanted him to see me as desirable and sexy.

"You can't begin to imagine how good it was to talk to you," Brent said. "I'll never forget you."

He let me go and stood back. "I really should leave," he said. "It's a long drive."

I nodded. "Yes, of course," I said. I felt so sad I thought I might cry. Brent had made me feel emotions that I hadn't felt in a long time. Now he was leaving. I would go back to my ordinary life, living alone in my big old house.

Brent went to the guest room and got his overnight bag. I followed him to the front porch to wave goodbye. Before he left, he rolled down his car window. "Tell me something, Annie," he said. "I'm curious. Why haven't you gone out with Steve?"

"You mean on a date?" I asked. "I don't know. I guess I just never saw Steve that way."

"You should take a second look," he said.

"After this weekend, I'm not sure I'll have the chance. I think my friendship with Steve may have come to an end."

"Oh, I think you'll see Steve later today," Brent said.

"Why do you say that?"

Brent pointed at the house behind me. "He left his toolbox by the front door."

Chapter Fourteen

Brent was right. Steve turned up later that afternoon.

"Annie, I've come for my toolbox," Steve called through the screen door. But I didn't bother to get up from the kitchen table. I was sitting there, sobbing into a Kleenex.

Steve opened the screen door and came inside. "What the hell's the matter with you?"

I turned my back to him so he wouldn't see my red face. "Nothing," I said.

"You can't tell me you're crying over nothing," he said. "This has something to do with that Brent character, doesn't it? Where is he, anyway? Is he going to be gone long? I came when I saw that his car was gone."

"He went back home," I said.

"Ah," Steve said. "That's why you're crying."

"No, that's not why I'm crying."

"Why, then?" he asked.

When I didn't answer, Steve poured us both a cup of coffee. He sat down at the kitchen table with me. He patted my hand. "There, there," he said.

"I really made a fool of myself this time," I said.

He raised his eyebrows at me. "Which moment are you speaking of?"

"Brent wasn't interested in me at all," I said. "He just wanted someone to talk to."

"Is that right?" Steve didn't sound surprised.

"You knew!"

"I figured he was the kind of man who is lost without the company of women," said Steve. "Men like that need a woman's attention or they fall apart. You were handy."

"Handy? You're saying I was simply convenient?"

"You said it yourself: he wanted someone to listen to him. You were there."

"He wanted someone to listen to him talk about losing his wife," I said. "She just passed away a few months ago."

That was news to Steve. I hadn't told him that Brent's wife had died only six months ago. He sat back in his chair to think for a moment. "I guess you can't fault him for wanting to talk about that," said Steve. "You've been there."

"Did you feel sort of used when I talked and talked about Joe after he died?" I asked.

"No, of course not," said Steve. "You needed to talk. Joe was my buddy, remember. I was also grieving at the time. Is that why you're crying? You feel used?"

I shook my head. "No."

"What then?"

"I'm crying because I'm all alone in this house. I'm tired of being alone."

"Is that all?" Steve leaned forward across the table. "Annie, you're the smartest woman I know. But sometimes you don't see what's right in front of your nose."

My Kleenex was wet, so I wiped my nose on my sleeve. I never would have done that in front of Brent. "What are you talking about?" I asked.

Steve didn't answer. He pulled me up from the table. Then he took me by the shoulders and pushed me gently towards the stairs. "Go upstairs and clean yourself up," he told me. "You have makeup all over your face."

"I do?" When I wiped under one eye, I found mascara on my finger. My tears must have made my eye makeup run.

"And put on something pretty," said Steve. "A dress, if you like. But make it something you can move in. Not that tight black dress you had on last night. You looked stuffed, like a sausage."

"That's a fine thing to say," I said, offended. "Especially right now."

"I didn't mean it that way," he said. "You were all curvy and sexy in that dress. You just looked uncomfortable. Now go put on something you feel at ease in."

"Why?"

"Just do it," he said. "I'll be back in one hour."

"Where are you going?" I called after him. "Are you taking me somewhere?"

But Steve didn't answer my questions. "Just get yourself ready," he told me. He left the house and jogged up the street to his place.

Chapter Fifteen

Steve was true to his word. He knocked on my door exactly one hour later. I hardly recognized him. He was freshly shaven. He smelled of expensive aftershave, and it wasn't the Old Spice he had worn the day before. His hair was neatly styled, combed away from his face, and he wore a nice suit.

"Wow!" I said. "Steve, is that you?"

"It's me."

"Honestly, you look so different," I said. "Now I'm not dressed up enough. Should I put something else on?" I wore a casual summer dress and sandals.

"No, you look perfect," he said. He took my hand. "Come on."

"Are we going to the Old Church Restaurant?" I asked.

"You went there last night, with *him*."

"Then where are you taking me? Where's your truck?"

"No need for the truck," he said. He led me down to the beach.

Steve had set up a table and two chairs right near the water. The table was covered with a tablecloth and set with plates and cutlery. A candle was lit inside a jar, so the wind wouldn't blow it out. A picnic basket sat beside it. Next to the table, Steve had set up his big telescope for looking at the stars.

"This is wonderful," I said.

Steve took both my hands. "Now, before dinner begins, I want to get something out of the way."

"What's that?" I asked.

"This." He took me in his arms and kissed me. His kiss made me tingle right down to my toes. We both stood back after that kiss, shocked at how it made us feel.

"Why didn't we do that before?" I asked him.

"My thought exactly," he said. "Annie, you already know we're good for each other. Just think how much you'd save on repair bills if we got together."

I laughed. "You've got a point," I said. "But don't you think we're moving too quickly? We haven't even had dinner."

"We've known each other for years," he said.

"I've only known you like *this* for a few minutes." I waved a hand at the new Steve in front of me. This Steve was handsome and confident. He was so handsome that I felt as nervous with him as I had with Brent.

"I want my old Steve back," I said. "Grubby, messy Steve. I felt comfortable with him."

"Give me a day and grubby Steve will be back," he said, running a hand over his chin.

We ate our picnic as the sun set. Then Steve showed me the rings of Saturn through his telescope. The planet and its rings looked like a diamond in the black sky. "I've never seen anything so beautiful," I said.

"I have," said Steve. He looked at me with such affection that I knew he meant me.

We gazed through the telescope at the stars and the moon until well after midnight. When it was time to go home, I helped Steve carry everything to his truck. He had parked in the beach parking lot.

Then Steve took my hand and walked me back to my bed and breakfast. As we drew close to home, both of us fell silent. I sensed the tension rise between us. When we reached the front steps of my house, I said, "Here we are."

"Here we are," Steve repeated. He tucked his hands in his pockets as he waited for me to ask him inside. When I hesitated a little too long, Steve said, "Well, goodnight." Disappointed and confused, he started to walk away.

"Steve, wait," I said.

"Yes?"

"There's something I'd like to offer you," I said. "I wouldn't, usually, after a first date. But as you said, we've known each other a long time."

"What's that?" Steve asked. He was already grinning. "What are you offering me?"

"A bed," I said. I grinned back at him. "And breakfast."

Good 📖 Reads

Discover Canada's Bestselling Authors with Good Reads Books

Good Reads authors have a special talent—
the ability to tell a great story, using clear language.

Good Reads can be purchased as eBooks, downloadable
direct to your mobile phone, eReader or computer.
Some titles are also available as audio books.

To find out more, please visit
www.GoodReadsBooks.com

The Good Reads project is supported by
ABC Life Literacy Canada.

Good Reads Series

All Night by Alan Cumyn

The Stalker by Gail Anderson-Dargatz

Coyote's Song by Gail Anderson-Dargatz

Bed and Breakfast by Gail Anderson-Dargatz

The Break-In by Tish Cohen

Tribb's Troubles by Trevor Cole

In From the Cold by Deborah Ellis

The Clear-Out by Deborah Ellis

New Year's Eve by Marina Endicott

Home Invasion by Joy Fielding

The Day the Rebels Came to Town by Robert Hough

Picture This by Anthony Hyde

Listen! by Frances Itani

Missing by Frances Itani

Shipwreck by Maureen Jennings

The Picture of Nobody by Rabindranath Maharaj

The Hangman by Louise Penny

Love You to Death by Elizabeth Ruth

Easy Money by Gail Vaz-Oxlade

Coyote's Song
by Gail Anderson-Dargatz

Sara used to be a back-up singer in a band. She left her singing career to raise a family. She is content with being a stay-at-home mom. Then, one Saturday, Sara's world changes.

Sara and her family go to an outdoor music festival. There, on stage, Sara sees Jim, the lead singer from her old band. He invites her to sing with him. Being on stage brings back forgotten feelings for Sara—and for Jim. And Sara's husband Rob sure doesn't like what he sees.

Sara also sees something else: a coyote. Learn how Coyote, the trickster spirit, turns Sara's life upside down.

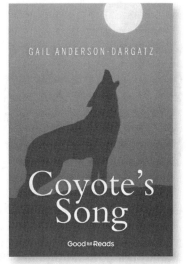

About the Author

 By the age of eighteen, Gail Anderson-Dargatz knew that she wanted to write about Canadian women in rural settings. Today, Gail is a bestselling author. *A Recipe for Bees* and *The Cure for Death by Lightning* were finalists for the Giller prize. She currently teaches fiction in the creative writing program at the University of British Columbia. Gail lives in the Shuswap region of BC, the landscape found in so much of her writing.

Also by Gail Anderson-Dargatz:

The Miss Hereford Stories
The Cure for Death by Lightning
A Recipe for Bees
A Rhinestone Button
Turtle Valley
The Stalker
Coyote's Song

*

You can visit Gail's website at
www.gailanderson-dargatz.ca